Ruby Rides an Elephant

Written by Ruby Lovell

Illustrated by Zara Merrick

ISBN: 978-1-9998685-0-5

Dedication

I dedicate this book to my sons Jacob and Monty
who learnt so much about their heritage and
absolutely loved their adventures in Sri Lanka.

Sri Lanka

Indian Ocean

Colombo

Ruby comes from a very special family.

Her mother is English and her father is Sri Lankan. That makes Ruby mixed race.

Ruby is very excited as she's going on a family holiday to her father's native country – the beautiful island of Sri Lanka for the first time. Her father has told her so many wonderful stories of growing up there and the amazing adventures she's going to have.

They leave for Sri Lanka tomorrow!

Ruby packed her bag for their trip. She was so excited as she'd never been to Sri Lanka before.

In her favourite backpack she put all the things she loved to keep with her. Fruits for when she got hungry. Her favourite comfy bear called Mala. Lots of paper and colouring pencils so she could draw everything she saw on their adventures.

After a long flight, they were finally in Sri Lanka. "Hooray!" squealed Ruby. She couldn't wait to start her adventure. Ruby's Dad was going to take her on a little trip around the island that weekend by car.

"You're in for a big surprise Ruby!" said her Daddy. Now Ruby was really excited. What could the surprise be? Were they going to the beach? Ruby loved the beach and always collected shells from each beach she went to. Maybe they were going to the zoo. She particularly loved the big cats in the zoo:

like the tigers **"RRRRRR!"**

and the lions **"RAAAAR!"**

and the snakes **"SSSSSSS!"**

"Tell me daddy please!" she squealed. "It's amazing, it's supreme. It's going to make you want to scream!!" he said.

They drove for a while and Ruby saw lots of interesting scenes from her window as they left the City. There were crowded buses. Even 3 wheeled cars called tuk tuks.

They had loud horns: BEEP BEEP BEEP
They heard, everytime they passed one.

Ladies in beautiful colour saris
   in pink,
      gold,
        green
          and blue.

She decided to make up a song:

"A tuk tuk here a tuk tuk there,
beep beep beep everywhere.
Lots of colours, cheery and bright.
It's an adventure. Oh that's right!" she sang.

9

Finally they reached their destination. 'We're here' said Dad. She looked out of her window. There she saw a...

GIGANTIC...
ENORMOUS...
HUGE...ELEPHANT!

Ruby's eyes opened wide. She stared at this enormous elephant.

"I told you you won't believe your eyes" said Dad.

"Come on, we're going to have a ride on it. When I was a little boy your age, growing up in Sri Lanka, my Daddy took me on an elephant ride too" said her Dad. "I loved it!"

Ruby jumped out of the car and they went closer.
"She's called Rani" said the friendly man who
was looking after her. "She's 60 years old.
Elephants can live to 80 years old you know".

"Why is she flapping her ears like that?" asked Ruby. "When elephants get very hot, that's how they cool themselves" he said. "They also spray water on their bodies to cool down".

"Wow Dad, Rani is huge!"

"That's because elephants spend 20 hours a day just eating! They eat grass, leaves and tree bark".

"She weighs the same as your school bus!" Ruby laughed.

"We're going to ride her just like I ride in my school bus!"

Ruby and her Dad climbed up a long staircase attached to a platform.
Once they got to the top, they were at the right level to climb onto Rani.

Rani had a big seat strapped to her back.

They climbed onto the seat and
once they were on, off they went.

14

"WHHHHOOW...it's rocky Dad" she squealed "and it's so high up here!"
"Hold on tight, Rani can go fast if you want her to" said the man.

15

Ruby held on tight and off they went,

STOMP.

STOMP.

STOMP,

through the forest trees
and up a steep hill and
in the river too.

16

She had the ride of her life.

17

To say thank you to Rani, Ruby fed her some bananas. Rani the elephant took them very gently by curling her long trunk around them.

She then pushed them into her mouth.

Ruby giggled as she'd never seen bananas eaten without being peeled first. "Rani must have been really hungry after giving us a ride" she said.

18

Ruby had a wonderful day discovering this beautiful island and meeting her new friend Rani. She couldn't wait for more adventures with her Dad.

But for now it was time for a big sleep!

Adventures are really tiring.

Acknowledgments

I would like to express my gratitude to my two sons, Jacob and Monty, who were the inspiration to write this book.

Now the adventures you had will be shared with the children who read this book.

A special thank you to my son Monty: you sat with me and created the captivating storylines and characters I drew from: you are super talented, creative and have a fantastic imagination.

To my mother Iris and brother Charles: you became the basis of my characters.

To the empathetic and committed staff at Pinnewala Elephant Orphanage in Sri Lanka: you care so well for the injured and needy elephants. You opened my eyes to the many different facets of an elephant.

Last, but not least, thank you to my literary agent, KT: your efforts and commitment are much appreciated.

Sri Lanka

Made in the USA
Monee, IL
03 February 2021

59375570R10017

Ruby is on a fantastic
holiday with her parents on
the tropical island of Sri Lanka.

What exciting adventures will
her parents take her on?

She certainly never expected to go on this ride:
NO not in a car, NO not on a bus – but on an
Elephant! Through forests, jungles and
lakes. Ruby also makes a new best
friend in Rani the Elephant.

http://www.lycheebooks.org/

£6.99